DETECTIVE MOSY
and the
FIENDISH FOUR

for Marta and Angela

DETECTIVE NOSY
and the
FIENDISH FOUR

Alex Randolph

Pictures by
Fabio Visintin

PUFFIN BOOKS

Here he is!
Norman Nosy is doing
his morning exercises.

He is very agile.
Also amazingly quick and alert.

All excellent qualities
for a famous
International Detective.

"I'll check in later," he calls to his mother
as he sets out for another hard day
of thief-catching.

Notice his bulging pockets.
Inside are the tools of his trade,
including a large magnifying glass,
an all-purpose Swiss army knife
and two smelly cheese-and-chocolate sandwiches.

A policeman rushes up to him.
"There you are, Sir! Hurry up!
They're all asking for you at Headquarters.
It's an emergency!"

But first he must make
a quick change of costume...

Because, like all International Detectives,
Norman Nosy is a Master of Disguise.

Here are a few of his favourite disguises:

1

2

3

4

5

6

7

8

9

10

11

12

13

14

15

16

17   18   19   20

21   22   23   24

25   26   27   28

29   30   31

But sometimes his disguise
is not quite appropriate for the occasion...

Such as here... Detective Nosy is
reporting to the Chief of Police.

The whole Headquarters is in a frenzy
because news has just come in
that the Fiendish Four
are on the loose again.

"My dear Detective," says the Chief of Police,
"first, you will kindly remove that ridiculous get-up.
And second, here is your task for the day:
apprehend the Fiendish Four!"

From the archives at Police Headquarters, here are mugshots of the Fiendish Four and other important records:

The Fiendish Four are celebrating their 12th escape from prison.

Notice their secret identifying mark - green noses.

And straightaway they're back at work.

Here they are, a minute
before an amazing robbery...

So perfect is their teamwork,
that in most cases their victims
don't even notice that they are being cleaned out.

And here a minute *after*...

But this time their crime did not go unnoticed.
Detective Nosy, disguised as a dustbin,
saw everything. "Now I must follow them
and find out where they stash the loot!"

The Fiendish Four are doing their famous
getaway-skip-step:

And Detective Nosy is not far behind, taking notes.

But something strange is going on.

The Fiendish Four don't seem to be in a hurry at all.

Why?

"He's still following us,"
says Fiendish Two.
"Now he's disguised as a tree!"

"And now he's disguised as a phone booth!"
says Fiendish Four.

But this time they made a mistake,
for Detective Nosy really *is* in a phone booth.

It's the time of day when he always talks
to his mother on the phone:

"Hello, hello. I'm checking in!"

"Now wait a moment - tell me, did you
eat your sandwiches?"

"Yes, of course. I also had some orange and
anchovy juice...   But now I have to go,
they are waiting for me..."

"They are? That's nice. Run along, then,
Norman, but don't catch cold!"

"At last!" thinks Detective Nosy. "This must be the Fiendish Four's loot-house. All the evidence points to it..."

Detective Nosy
bursts in in fine style:
"You're all under arrest!"
he announces.

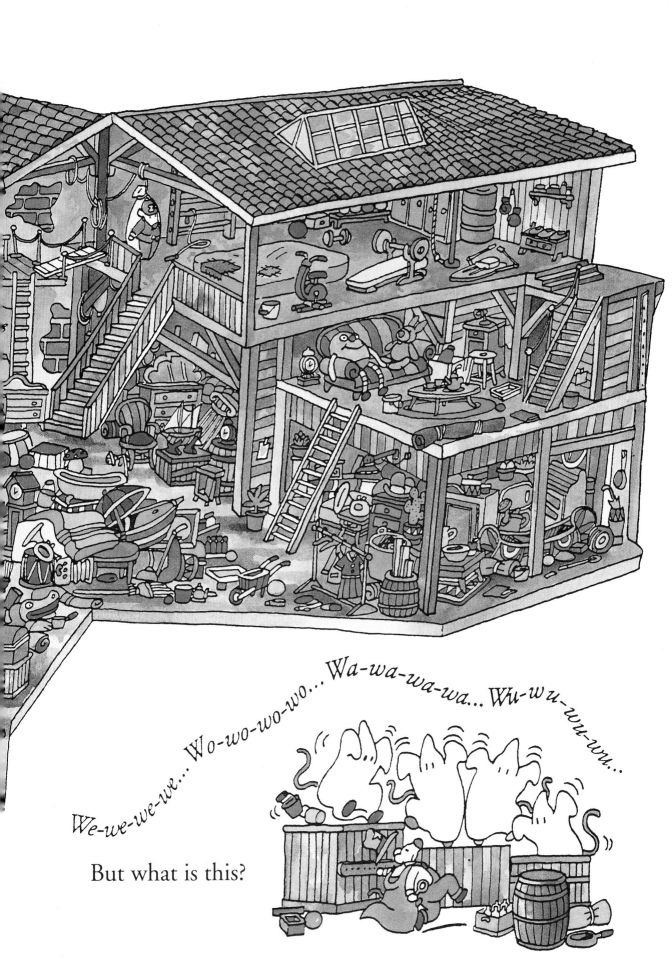

We-we-we-we... Wo-wo-wo-wo... Wa-wa-wa-wa... Wu-wu-wu-wu...

But what is this?

"Ghosts!...
    They're after me!"

"Help! Help!" he cries. "Fiendish Four, where are you?
Help me! Help me!"

"Here we are!"

He tries to escape, but where to?

"Fooled you this time!" they shout.

But Detective Nosy begins to cry:

"That wasn't nice of you," he sobs.
"I was supposed to arrest you.
Now what am I going to do?"

The Fiendish Four crowd around him.

"Please don't cry, Detective Nosy! - please!"...
"We were only joking" ... "Come on, of course
you can arrest us, go ahead!" ... "We don't mind
going back to jail..."

"Besides, we can always escape again,
whenever we want to!"

And so Detective Nosy returns
to Police Headquarters in triumph,
bringing back not only the Fiendish Four,
but their loot, too!

"Well done, Detective Nosy,"
says the Chief of Police.

After that
there is a wonderful party
with spinach ice-cream
for everybody.

But where
is Detective Nosy?

He is on the phone to his mother.

"Yes, I'll be coming home soon."

"Good. And tell me, Norman, what did you do today?"

"Me? Oh, nothing much... You know, the usual things... I'll tell you later."